Phonics Friends

Quana and Quinn
The Sound of Q

The
Child's
World

By Cecilia Minden and Joanne Meier

The Child's World

Published in the United States of America
by The Child's World®
PO Box 326
Chanhassen, MN 55317-0326
800-599-READ
www.childsworld.com

The Child's World®: Mary Berendes, Publishing Director

A special thank you to the Rodriquez and Nevarez
families. Alex and Anaiz, may your dreams of "new
things to be" come true.

Editorial Directions, Inc.: E. Russell Primm, Editorial
Director and Project Editor; Katie Marsico, Associate
Editor; Judith Shiffer, Associate Editor and School Media
Specialist; Linda S. Koutris, Photo Researcher and
Selector

The Design Lab: Kathleen Petelinsek, Design and Page
Production

Photographs ©: Photo setting and photography by Romie
and Alice Flanagan/Flanagan Publishing Services.

Library of Congress Cataloging-in-Publication Data
Minden, Cecilia.
  Quana and Quinn : the sound of Q / by Cecilia
Minden and Joanne Meier.
    p. cm. — (Phonics friends)
  Summary: Simple text featuring the sound of the letter
"q" describes the activities of Quana and her little
brother Quinn.
  ISBN 1-59296-303-X (library bound : alk. paper) [1.
English language—Phonetics. 2. Reading.] I. Minden,
Cecilia. II. Title. III. Series.
PZ7.M5148Qu 2004
[E]—dc22   2004003537

Note to parents and educators:

The Child's World® has created Phonics Friends with the goal of exposing children to engaging stories and pictures that assist in phonics development. The books in the series will help children learn the relationships between the letters of written language and the individual sounds of spoken language. This contact helps children learn to use these relationships to read and write words.

The books in this series follow a similar format. An introductory page, to be read by an adult, introduces the child to the phonics feature, or sound, that will be highlighted in the book. Read this page to the child, stressing the phonic feature. Help the student learn how to form the sound with her mouth. The Phonics Friends story and engaging photographs follow the introduction. At the end of the story, word lists categorize the feature words into their phonic element. Additional information on using these lists is on The Child's World® Web site listed at the top of this page.

Each book in this series has been carefully written to meet specific readability requirements. Close attention has been paid to elements such as word count, sentence length, and vocabulary. Readability formulas measure the ease with which the text can be read and understood. Each Phonics Friends book has been analyzed using the Spache readability formula. For more information on this formula, as well as the levels for each of the books in this series please visit The Child's World® Web site.

Reading research suggests that systematic phonics instruction can greatly improve students' word recognition, spelling, and comprehension skills. The Phonics Friends series assists in the teaching of phonics by providing students with important opportunities to apply their knowledge of phonics as they read words, sentences, and text.

This is the letter *q*.

In this book, you will read words that
have the *q* sound as in:

   queen, quick, quiet, and *quilt.*

Quana likes to pretend.

Her little brother, Quinn,

does too.

Sometimes Quana is a queen.

She wears a crown.

Quinn is the king.

He feels quite important!

Sometimes Quana is a doctor.

She wants to care for Quinn.

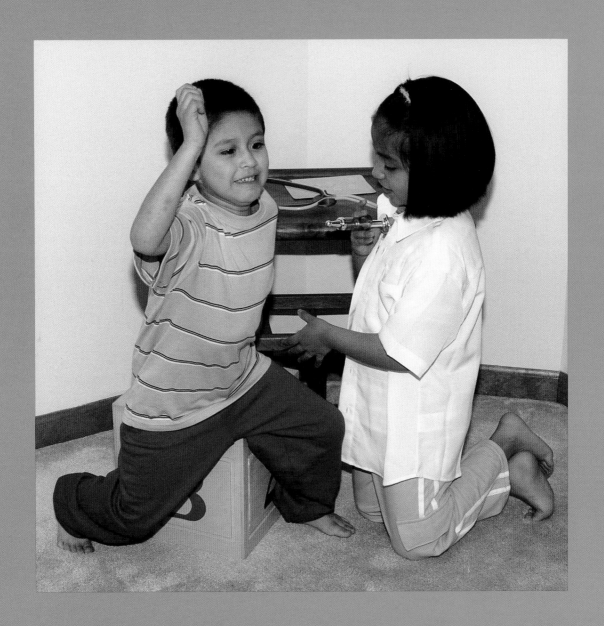

Quinn is too quick.

He runs away!

It is time for bed.

It is time to be quiet.

Quana sleeps under a warm quilt. Quinn sleeps, too.

Quana and Quinn will be quiet and sleep. They will dream of new things to be.

Fun Facts

Many kings are married to queens, but one was married to six! Between 1509 and 1547, King Henry VIII of England was married to six different women. Four were from England, one was from Spain, and one was from Germany. Henry's daughter, Queen Elizabeth I, was the first queen to own a wristwatch. Elizabeth was the daughter of Henry's second wife, Queen Anne Boleyn.

You probably already know that sleeping under a quilt can be quite cozy, but did you know that some people think it brings good luck? Supposedly, any dreams you have the first night you sleep under a new quilt are likely to come true! Some quilters are also very careful not to break any thread as they work. They believe this could bring bad luck.

Activity

Designing Your Own Quilt

It might be difficult for you to make your own quilt without the help of an adult, but there's no reason you can't design one! With crayons or markers, divide a piece of paper into 25 squares. Decide what colors and shapes you would pick for each square. When you are finished, keep the design in a safe place for when you are ready to make your own quilt. Or perhaps a family member with experience making quilts would be willing to help you put one together based on your design!

To Learn More

Books
About the Sound of Q

Klingel, Cynthia, and Robert B. Noyed. *Quack!: The Sound of Q.* Chanhassen,
  Minn.: The Child's World, 2000.

About Queens

Engelbreit, Mary. *Queen of Christmas.* New York: HarperCollins, 2003.

Marnis, Celeste Davidson, and Bagram Ibatoulline (illustrator). *The Queen's
  Progress.* New York: Viking, 2003.

O'Neill, Alexis, and Laura Huliska-Beith (illustrator). *The Recess Queen.* New
  York: Scholastic, 2002.

About Quilts

Brumbeau, Jeff, and Gail De Marcken (illustrator). *Quiltmaker's Gift.* Duluth,
  Minn.: Pfeifer-Hamilton Publishers, 2000.

Polacco, Patricia. *The Keeping Quilt.* New York: Simon & Schuster Books for
  Young Readers, 1998.

Root, Phyllis, and Margot Apple (illustrator). *The Name Quilt.* New York:
  Farrar, Straus and Giroux, 2003.

Web Sites
Visit our home page for lots of links about the Sound of Q:

http://www.childsworld.com/links.html

Note to Parents, Teachers, and Librarians: We routinely check our Web links to make
sure they're safe, active sites—so encourage your readers to check them out!

Q Feature Words

Proper names

Quana

Quinn

**Feature Words in
Initial Position**

queen

quick

quiet

quilt

quite

About the Authors

Cecilia Minden, PhD, directs the Language and Literacy Program at the Harvard Graduate School of Education. She is a reading specialist with classroom and administrative experience in grades K–12. She earned her PhD in reading education from the University of Virginia. Cecilia and her husband Dave Cupp enjoy sharing their love of reading with their granddaughter Chelsea.

Joanne Meier, PhD, has worked as an elementary school teacher and university professor. She earned her BA in early childhood education from the University of South Carolina, and her MEd and PhD in education from the University of Virginia. She currently works as a literacy consultant for schools and private organizations. Joanne Meier lives with her husband Eric, and spends most of her time chasing her two daughters, Kella and Erin, and her two cats, Sam and Gilly, in Charlottesville, Virginia.